# WOMEN WARRIORS

## *Myths and Legends of Heroic Women*

### MARIANNA MAYER

ILLUSTRATED BY
### JULEK HELLER

MORROW JUNIOR BOOKS
*New York*

Watercolors were used for the full-color illustrations.
The text type is 12-point Galliard.

Published by Morrow Junior Books
a division of William Morrow and Company, Inc.
1350 Avenue of the Americas, New York, NY 10019
www.williammorrow.com

Printed in Singapore at Tien Wah Press.

1   3   5   7   9   10   8   6   4   2

Library of Congress Cataloging-in-Publication Data
Mayer, Marianna.
Women warriors: myths and legends of heroic women / Marianna Mayer; illustrated by Julek Heller.
p.  cm.
Summary: A collection of twelve traditional tales about female
military leaders, war goddesses, women warriors, and heroines from
around the world, including such countries as Japan, Ireland, and Zimbabwe.
ISBN 0-688-15522-7
1. Women heroes—Folklore.   2. Tales.   [1. Heroes—Folklore.
2. Women—Folklore.   3. Folklore.]   I. Heller, Julek, ill.   II. Title.
PZ8.1.M46Wo 1999   398'.082—dc21   98-45697   CIP  AC

# CONTENTS

# INTRODUCTION

There was once a warrior maiden who was told that her actions were like those of a man. "If I do these things, then they must be the ways of a woman," she replied, "since that is what I know myself to be."

The heroines portrayed in this collection prove her point. Riding horses as though born to it, using weapons with consummate skill, and leading their lives with passion, they often inspired thousands to follow. These are spirited women warriors from different times, cultures, and social classes who embody the kind of forthrightness we have come to think that only modern women possess. They are far from the meek heroines—often in desperate need of a hero—found in many traditional fairy tales and folktales, and they are unlike the submissive or oppressed women described in much of the fiction and history of centuries past.

For all their bravery and love of adventure, they are complex and often disturbing women who defy one-dimensional analysis. In the dangerous, sometimes barbaric times in which they lived, these women could be ruthless, bloodthirsty, and even vengeful. Whether or not their actions were admirable poses an interesting question and provides opportunity for lively discussion. But whatever else might be said for them, these female heroes willingly took responsibility for their deeds, regardless of the consequences, and never made apologies.

These twelve profiles were pulled from a vast store of historical and literary material that was often incomplete and contradictory and at times was told from the point of view of the warrior's opponents—making the creation of the profiles like sifting through and piecing together broken fragments unearthed from an archaeological dig. Some, like the Celtic Scathach (the inspiration for the Lady Lochlyn) and Hiera of the nation of Amazons, were created from scant threads of legend. Others, such as Semiramis of Assyria and Boadicea of the Iceni, the solitary women in command of their armies, were inspired by rich historical sources. A few of the women included, such as the devoted Yakami from Japan (also known as Li Chi in China) and the determined Mella from Zimbabwe, are much better known in their own cultures than they are in the wider world. Perhaps the best preserved are the myths concerning warrior goddesses like the Celtic Morrigan and the Hindu goddess Devi (or Durga).

Considerations of space made the inclusion of countless other female heroes impossible. Their stories, just as compelling, include the already well-documented lives of Cleopatra and Joan of Arc; or the more obscure Septimia Zenobia, queen of Palmyra (an ancient city northeast of Damascus), who challenged Rome in the third century A.D.; Camilla, who was hailed for her warrior skill by Virgil in the *Aeneid;* and Nzinga Mbande, the seventeenth-century queen of Angola.

Rather than a celebration of war, these tales are a tribute to the commitment and courage of each heroine as well as an exploration of the nature and uses of the innate power of womanhood. Here are the stories of twelve women who understood that power and were willing to fight—sometimes to the death—for what they believed in.

# A NOTE ABOUT PRONUNCIATION

The spelling and pronunciation of ancient names can be challenging and confusing, since the stories in which they appear have often been passed down through the oral tradition (or they originated in a language that was written in a non-Western alphabet or perhaps was not written at all). For ease in reading, the simplest or most common version of each woman's name is used. Keep in mind that in further reading there may be many variations. For example, Boadicea is also spelled Boudicca, Voadicea, Boodicia, Bunduica, Bunduca, Bonduica, and Voadicia, and Morrigan is also referred to as Morrigu, Muirgen, Morrigaine, or Morgan.

| | |
|---|---|
| Aliquipiso | ah-li-QUI-peh-soh |
| Boadicea | bow-di-SEE-a |
| Devi | DAY-vee |
| Gwendolen | GWEN-doh-len |
| Hiera | HEER-rah |
| Mella | MEE-lah |
| Morrigan | MOR-ree-an |
| Rangada | rahn-GAH-dah |
| Scathach | SCATH |
| Semiramis | sem-ee-RAM-us |
| Winyan Ohitika | WEE-yahn oh-HEE-tee-kah |
| Yakami | YAH-kah-mee |

# Some WOMEN·WARRIORS

Freya · Brunnhilda · BOADICEA · SCATHACH · Scotland · Sweden · Olga · Russia · Alvild · A S · MORRIGAN · Ireland · Britain · Netherlands · Isabella Clara Eugenia · Kenau & Amaron Haselaar · Wales · London · Schwarze Hofmannin · GWENDOLEN · Germany · EUROPE · Brunehaut · France · Sarka · Frédégonde · Caterina Sforz · Spain · Italy · Rome · BLACK SEA · Tamara · Georgia · Amazonia · Catalina de Erauso · MEDITERRANEAN SEA · Ionia Turkey · HIERA · Aegean Sea · Asia Minor · Assyria · SEMIRAMIS · Damia al-Kahina · Babylon · Anat · Raziya · Ankt · RANGADA · Egypt · Arabia · Septimia Zenobia · India · DEVI · AFRICA · Nigeria · Ethiopia · Amina Sarauniya Zazzua · INDIAN OCEAN · Nzinga Mbande · ATLANTIC · Angola · OCEAN · MELLA · Zimbabwe

Here are the names of a few female military leaders, war goddesses, and heroines from around the world. The stories of the women whose names appear in capital letters are told in this collection. For more information

10

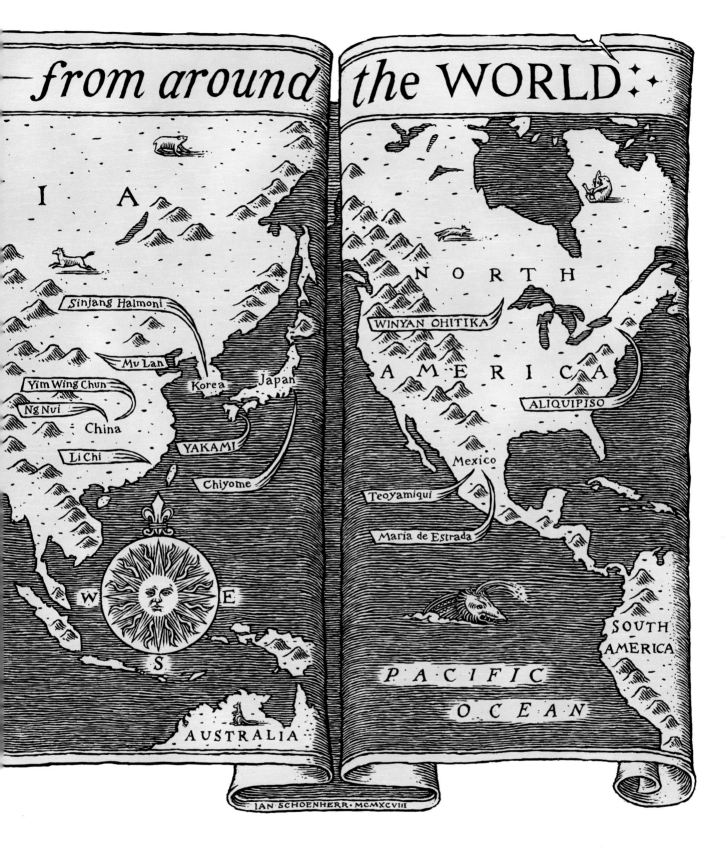

*on the others, please refer to the index on page 78. (Countries, cities, and regions noted on the map are those mentioned in the book. Words in italic are ancient place names no longer in use.)*

# DEVI

## THE GODDESS WHO
## CONQUERED THE EVIL ONE

*Devi is the Sanskrit word for "deity" or "goddess."*
*Its literal meaning is "glowing with radiant light."*
*This story of Devi, who possessed one thousand arms, and her*
*great battle with the evil Durga comes from the collection*
*of East Indian stories called the* Puranas.

Many lifetimes ago the name of Durga was the name of all that was evil. Indeed, Durga was once known as the supreme Evil One. Taking the form of the colossal Mahisa buffalo, he drove the deities out of the heavens, forcing them to seek shelter in earthly forests. But Durga followed them, smashing all the holy places where the sacred were worshiped. Still not content, the buffalo demon stole the flames from hearth fires, diverted rivers, and caused droughts and floods. He tore up mountains with his great buffalo horns and captured many goddesses, forcing each perfect being to work as his slave.

The people beseeched the great god Shiva, begging him to rid them of the Evil One. But Shiva could not, for his power was not as great as the demon buffalo's. So Shiva called upon the goddess Devi and said, "Golden One, you alone have the power and energy of the world in your grasp. Only you can defeat the demon that is terrorizing your people."

But Devi was busy with many different tasks, and so she sent dark Kalatri, guardian of the night, to take up the battle. But alas, Kalatri was quickly defeated. Only Devi had the strength to vanquish the demon.

So at last Devi mounted her giant tiger and rode out to challenge Durga. But the demon was armed with one hundred and twenty million elephants, an equal number of war chariots, and troops beyond counting. All these lay in wait for battle with Devi, and as she approached, an avalanche of arrows fell upon her. Yet Devi passed through them as if they were a cloud of harmless gnats. Then the army hurled great boulders. These fell away from Devi's body like harmless grains of sand. The buffalo demon snorted in anger, and his breath stirred up hurricanes, uprooted trees, and wiped out forests. Yet Devi advanced.

Outraged, the demon buffalo began to lash his tail, and suddenly the oceans swelled and tidal waves rose up and crashed down upon the land. Still, Devi advanced.

In wild frustration the demon fell upon Devi's tiger. Devi lassoed his buffalo tail, but it slipped free as the demon melted into the form of an enormous lion. Devi drove her sword into the demon lion's neck, but in an instant it changed into an armed warrior. Devi shot her bow and an arrow pushed past the shape changer's sword and shield, piercing his heart. Now the demon became an elephant.

The world was ravaged by the furious fighting. Yet as battle after battle continued, no one won and no one lost, until the demon took on his true form to challenge Devi. Stripped of all his disguises, the demon finally faced the warrior goddess as Durga the Evil One, and he too had one thousand arms. In hand-to-hand combat the two clashed. Then silently Devi drew back. Seeing this, the people wept, for they believed that she, their only hope, was ready to admit defeat.

Devi took up a cup of blood-red wine and slowly drank. As she did, Durga laughed in triumph, assuming victory. "You may laugh," said Devi, rising to her full height, "but not for long."

Then, finishing the last drop of the heavenly wine, with lightning speed Devi raised her foot and let it crash down on the demon's neck. Devi now plunged her golden trident into Durga's body over and over again until the demon lay lifeless.

Delivered from peril, the world rejoiced. The people gave their victorious champion the name of her opponent in memory of the great cosmic battle, thus calling the goddess Devi also Durga. This way throughout the rest of time those speaking of Durga would forever remember that his colossal power was but a part of the great Devi.

# RANGADA
## Noble Leader of Her Tribe

*This little-known story about a mortal woman named
Rangada can be found in the epic seventeen-volume work of
ninety thousand stanzas entitled the* Mahabharata. *Hindu
tradition dates it at 3000* B.C., *while some scholars of Indian
literature suggest 900* B.C. *or even as late as 300* B.C.

Rangada, the warrior maiden, rode her horse with courage
burning in her dark eyes. Her arrows never missed, she drove
off invading enemies fearlessly, and none of her fellow tribesmen could match her remarkable skill. The tribe made Rangada its
leader, for it would have been impossible to choose one better.

The forthright Rangada never held back and always spoke her
mind. So when she came upon the renowned bowman Arjuna asleep
beneath a tree, she boldly approached, though she did not know who
he was. Struck by the handsome stranger, Rangada drew nearer. The
sound of her footsteps upon the dry leaves awakened Arjuna, and he
reached for his bow.

"Handsome youth," said Rangada without a trace of shyness,
"never before have I seen a man as beautiful as you. Your every feature
is flawless. I have not felt love for anyone, but I could love you with my
whole heart."

Arjuna was stunned by the outspoken girl. "I am not looking for a
mate," he told her quickly, "for I am sworn to a year of solitude." This
was true, but the hero then added, "Still, if I were free, I would not
choose a maiden whose bow and arrows tell of a life that I have been
brought up to believe is not fitting for a woman."

His words stung Rangada to the heart. Though Arjuna had

spurned her, she left still full of love for him. When she arrived home, Rangada threw off her hunting clothes and wrapped herself in flowing silks. Casting her bow and arrows aside, she adorned her wrists and ankles with golden bangles. She put on jeweled hoop earrings and rubbed sweet-smelling oils onto her almond-colored skin. Then she made her way back to Arjuna's tent. There she found him lost in meditation. She quietly entered the tent and sat upon a mat to wait. When Arjuna looked up, the sight of Rangada startled him. Now she was beautiful to his eyes, and he sat down beside her, never imagining that this beauty and the huntress he had met earlier were one and the same.

Taking her hand, Arjuna said, "Surely you are no mortal, but some perfect nymph or goddess, for how else could such a splendid beauty so mysteriously appear before me?" Filled with happiness, Rangada gave him a serene smile, deciding to say nothing of her true identity.

So it was that Arjuna broke his vow of solitude for Malha, for that was the name Rangada called herself while she was with him. For thirteen months Arjuna and Malha lived together joyfully. They walked along the mossy banks of the river hand and hand and bathed in the crystal-clear water. They gathered soft green ferns for their bed in the warm summer nights and slept wrapped in each other's arms when the evenings grew cool. In that time Arjuna hunted for their food, and Malha cooked for the man she loved.

But in the fourteenth month a group of tribesmen came to Arjuna's tent, searching for their leader. They spoke of a brave-hearted girl at the peak of her strength and beauty, a maiden skilled at all weaponry, who rode as one with her wild raven-black steed, and whose courage had no bounds. As he listened, Arjuna, the great warrior, wondered at the possibility of a woman capable of being his equal in all things. Imagining riding side by side with her, he suddenly longed to know her.

"Since Rangada has disappeared," the tribesmen continued, "we have been besieged by our enemies. Our villages have been raided, and our tents burned. Without our great leader we are powerless to fight off these invaders. If she is indeed lost to us, we shall all perish."

Pitying them, Arjuna said, "If you wish, I will ride with you against your enemies."

All the while Rangada had been listening from inside the tent. At last, unable to deny her people, she stepped out. Knowing that she risked Arjuna's rejection and anger for having concealed her identity, Rangada offered her help. With cries of joy her comrades reached out their hands to touch her, and some fell to their knees at the welcome sight of their noble leader. Astonished, Arjuna stood apart from the jubilant reunion in silence.

As Rangada mounted her wild steed, Arjuna marveled at the sight of his gentle Malha, for suddenly he saw that she had the strength and skill to calm the animal. Indeed, he could barely trust his own eyes, for here was a warrior in all ways fierce yet womanly. Then Rangada called to her beloved Arjuna, inviting him to join the upcoming battle. With a sense of excitement that surprised even him, Arjuna quickly mounted his horse and went to ride by the side of the woman he loved.

# SEMIRAMIS

## CHILD OF THE DOVES

*Queen Sammuramat of Assyria is best known by her
Greek name, Semiramis. Although she is the earliest female
warrior whose existence has some certainty, scholars differ greatly on the
specific date of her reign, with varying opinions spanning some 1,535
years. According to one Roman scholar, she lived about 2177 B.C., while
the Greek historian Herodotus suggested a reign as late as 713 B.C.
However, there is no debate over the fact that the childhood of
this real-life queen is the stuff of mythological legend.*

One morning in late summer the goddess Derceto, heavy with child, stepped into the wildwood near Ascalon in Syria. There, all alone, she gave birth. Later that day only the wild creatures of the forest heard an abandoned baby's feeble cries. A flock of doves drawn by the sound gathered in the branches of the trees overhead. "If we don't find food for the little one, she will surely starve to death," observed one.

"Surely the mother will be back," said another.

But when night fell and there was no sign of the mother, one dove said, "It breaks my heart to listen to the infant's cries."

"It will be cold tonight," said another.

So the doves made a nest for the infant and fed her berries and nectar of wildflowers.

The next day the birds went to Sisona, the shepherd of King Ninus' royal flock. Sisona and his wife were an elderly couple with a cottage on the edge of the wood. Out of their meager provisions this kindly pair always found food for the birds and other wild creatures. That morning the doves tap, tap, tapped at the cottage window.

Though Sisona and his wife did not understand, they stepped out-doors to see what was the matter. *"Come with us!"* the birds cooed, pulling at the old shepherd's cap and his wife's apron strings.

Clearly the birds wanted them to follow, so the old couple did just that. As soon as the doves saw this, they set off into the wood. At last they came upon the infant in a down-feathered nest.

"Oh," cried the old woman, "what a beautiful baby! Surely the doves mean for us to look after her."

Sisona and his wife brought the child home. Having no children of their own, they were overjoyed and adopted the babe, giving her the name Semiramis, which means "dove."

As the months slipped into years, the lovely child grew into a care-free young woman. No one knew Semiramis was the daughter of a goddess, but anyone seeing her out in the woodland with the wild creatures she loved would have supposed she was too beautiful to be a mortal.

One day Menon, the king's principal officer, came to inspect the royal flock under Sisona's care. Captivated by Semiramis' surpassing beauty and charming conversation, the young man thereafter made many visits. At last the officer begged her to marry him. When she consented, Menon took Semiramis to his palace in the capital city of Nineveh.

For many months they lived happily, but Menon kept his bride hidden from society, fearing that if any man saw her, he would have to fight to the death to keep her. But Semiramis was too brilliant and strong-willed to be content to live in seclusion, even if such a life was filled with every luxury. When war broke out and Menon was called to fight, Semiramis insisted on joining him.

At first one city after another fell to the Assyrians. Then in Media, at the seemingly impenetrable wall of Bactria, the army came to a standstill. Unable to scale the well-defended fortress, King Ninus of Assyria ordered his forces to retreat. That night Semiramis surprised everyone by going before Ninus and his assembled war council to propose a cleverly devised assault on the fortress. "But no one will volunteer to lead such a raid. It is suicide!" declared the councillors.

"I will lead your troops, Majesty," Semiramis said. So impressed was the king that he endorsed her plan.

When the decisive moment arrived, Semiramis proved herself fully equal to the task. Amid a barrage of arrows and stones, before which the bravest men trembled, she led her troops to the foot of the citadel. The sight of a beautiful woman braving the same dangers that caused them to pale united the soldiers. Ignoring the peril, they followed the intrepid heroine, who rushed up the scaling ladder and was the first to reach the battlements. A fierce but brief fight ensued, and soon the Assyrian flag was raised from the top of the great wall.

Now Ninus was overcome with desire for the beautiful warrior and urged her husband to give her up to him. When Menon refused, Ninus in a fury had him blinded and imprisoned. Deprived of his beloved Semiramis, Menon died mysteriously in his cell shortly after.

The king married the young widow, but he paid dearly for the honor. While in his royal court Semiramis won the hearts of the courtiers and the army alike. In no time she was the supreme power of Assyria. She cast Ninus into prison and later put him to death to avenge the loss of Menon.

Queen Semiramis had a long and prosperous reign. She founded Babylon, which was called the Golden City, and designed the famed Hanging Gardens of Babylon, one of the Seven Wonders of the Ancient World. Not satisfied with the vast empire left by Ninus, she enlarged it by successive conquests. A great part of Ethiopia came under her power. Remarkably Semiramis was the only sovereign among the ancients, except Alexander the Great, who ever carried a war beyond the Indus River.

In old age Semiramis voluntarily abdicated the throne to her son. She lived sixty-two years, out of which she reigned as queen for forty-two. It is said the Athenians thereafter worshiped her as a goddess in the form of a pure white dove, and others thought of her as another form of the goddess Astarte.

*A bronze statue of Semiramis armed with a sword was once supported upon lofty pillars. One such pillar remains, engraved with the queen's own words:*

NATURE MADE ME A WOMAN YET I HAVE RAISED MYSELF TO RIVAL THE GREATEST MEN. I SWAYED THE SCEPTER OF NINOS; I EXTENDED MY DOMINIONS TO THE RIVER HINAMEMES EASTWARD; TO THE SOUTHWARD TO THE LAND OF FRANKINCENSE AND MYRRH; NORTHWARD TO SACCAE AND SCYTHIANS. NO ASSYRIAN BEFORE ME HAD SEEN AN OCEAN, BUT I HAVE SEEN FOUR. I HAVE BUILT DAMS AND FERTILIZED THE BARREN LAND WITH MY RIVERS. I HAVE BUILT IMPREGNABLE WALLS AND ROADS TO FAR PLACES AND WITH IRON CUT PASSAGES THROUGH MOUNTAINS WHERE PREVIOUSLY EVEN WILD ANIMALS COULD NOT PASS. VARIOUS AS WERE MY DEEDS, I HAVE YET FOUND LEISURE HOURS TO INDULGE MYSELF WITH FRIENDS.

# A NOTE ABOUT
# AMAZON WARRIORS

*There are those who believe that once there was a nation
called Amazonia populated entirely by women. Legend tells that
for four hundred years (1000–600 B.C.) they held power over the portion
of Asia Minor bordering the shores of the Black Sea. The Amazons were
a race that devoted themselves entirely to developing their skills as
warriors. On certain days of each year, however, they set aside their
military pursuits and visited the surrounding settlements to
choose mates. Once children were born, the sons were left with
their fathers while the daughters returned with their
mothers to Amazonia to be instructed in the arts
of warfare, hunting, and riding.*

*It is thought that at the height of its
power Amazonia extended over all Asia Minor and
Ionia (an ancient region on the west coast of what is now
Turkey, including nearby islands in the Aegean),
as well as the greater part of Italy.*

# HIERA

## THE AMAZON QUEEN AND
## HER BITTER VICTORY

*Though a few Amazons are known by name—such as Marpesia,
Orithya, and Penthesilea—no complete tales of their conquests remain.
The following story of a brave Amazon queen is inspired by the scant
fragmented legends left to us by such early writers as Herodotus, known
by ancients and many moderns alike as the Father of History.*

Hiera, one of the Amazon queens, rode at the head of her army of women warriors for many years. Hiera was so fleet of foot that she could run through a field of wheat without damaging a blade or race across a river without wetting the soles of her feet. A brave warrior and a wise queen, Hiera was born with the mettle to face grim fights.

Even as a girl Hiera was regal, whether splendidly clothed in royal purple or dressed in leather armor. A golden brooch clasped her heavy, long black hair, and she wore a quiver of arrows and carried a fir wood staff with a bronze lance's head.

It is said that once a mighty king bent on conquering neighboring lands tried to gain her territories by offering marriage. Hiera declined, for the queen was well aware that he was wooing not her but her dominions. Instead she urged him to go in peace. But as she watched the bridges being built that would enable his armies to cross the river and begin an assault on her people, Hiera sent this message: "Rule your own people, and try to bear the sight of me ruling mine."

But peace was scarcely the aim of this power-hungry king. Within twenty years he had amassed a huge empire by conquering others. In response to Hiera's message, he offered to discuss a settlement at a banquet that he would provide. Going in good faith, Hiera's daughter Zedna, the general of her army, and other chief warriors attended. There the Amazons, after a lavish feast, were slaughtered, and the queen's daughter was captured.

Now the queen sent word to the king: "Hungry as you are for blood, you have no cause to be proud of your recent treachery, for it has no mark of military courage. Return my daughter, and leave my country." She continued grimly: "Refuse, and I vow to give you more blood than you have ever hungered for."

When the king ignored her ultimatum, Hiera saw to it that her words were horribly fulfilled. She and her troops swept down upon the enemy in a confrontation more violent than any other before fought between two nations. The queen, who had sought to mediate rather than go to war, now exulted amid the battle. Hiera and her faithful female warriors made the river echo with their hoofbeats as they rode their chariots of war, waving crescent shields and shrieking wild battle cries.

In her combat with the king Hiera battered through his shield and armor. At last, seeing her opportunity, she drove her shafted spear through his chest into his heart. "Did you imagine that you were chasing wild beasts in the forest?" she shouted. "Well, the day has come to prove that you imagined wrongly. Go to Hades with this message for your forefathers: You have earned some degree of distinction in your otherwise ignoble existence for having been slain by the hand of Hiera."

The Amazon queen and her army had succeeded in defeating their adversaries, but for Hiera it was a bitter victory. The queen soon discovered that her daughter was dead, having chosen suicide rather than endure captivity.

Before returning home, Hiera ordered a search to be made among the dead for the body of the king. When it was dragged before her, she took hold of the head of the corpse and plunged it into a skin filled with human blood, saying as she did, "Though I have conquered you and lived, still you have mortally wounded me by treacherously taking my daughter. See now—I fulfill my promise: Drink deep, greedy king, for at last you have more than your fill of blood."

# SCATHACH

## The Warriors' Teacher

*Stories of Amazon warriors spread beyond continental
Europe and Asia Minor. Ancient Celtic legend tells that if a
promising youth dared go to the island of Scathach the Amazon,
and learn her warrior craft, no man would be able to stand against
him. There, on what is usually identified as the isle of Skye, Scathach
trained some of the most famous warriors of the Celtic heroic
age. Among her specialties were pole vaulting, underwater
fighting, and combat with barbed harpoon, which she invented.
She was also described as a goddess, sage, poet, and prophet.*

*Though only fragmented legends relating to Scathach
remain, among the tales of King Arthur there is a woman in
the winter of her years who was said to select promising knights to
instruct in weaponry, courage, and compassion. Though she had
many names, her origins harken back to Scathach herself. In my tale
she is called the Lady Lochlyn, and the knight she has chosen is
named Ewain, son of the mistress of magic Morgan le Fay.*

Tell me, my son, are you a good fighter?" asked the Lady
Lochlyn when Ewain arrived at her camp.

"No, my lady, I am not experienced, and my strength is not
great," he answered. "I have won a few rounds while on the tilting field
against young men, and lost more."

"Good," said the lady. "Very good."

"*Good!* Why good?" asked the astonished youth.

"Because you have not yet made a habit of your faults. And I can
see by your movements that you were born with natural grace. It's

with such material that I can work best. And so I welcome you to my camp.”

The youth looked at the lady. Her hair was white, and her years were written plainly on her sunburned face. Her nose was strong like a hawk’s beak, and her amber eyes were farseeing and fierce.

The lady caught Ewain’s glance and gave him a wry smile. “You’re wondering how it is that a lady can be about such work, but you are too polite to ask.”

“Yes, ma’am, pardon. I mean no disrespect,” said the youth, and his face turned crimson.

“Never mind that, I will tell you,” she said. “As a little girl I hated those ladylike tasks given to girls: embroidery, lacemaking, and the like. Enviously I watched my brothers practicing their sports and cursed the gowns and dainty shoes that kept me from the free movement they took for granted. I knew I was a better rider then they, a better bow-man, and better with the spear, as I was to prove. So secretly I some-times dressed in my brothers’ clothes, and masked myself as well, and then went out into the forest like any young boy to await the chance to challenge whoever came along. I beat everyone I encountered, whether it was by wrestling or sword and shield. But then I killed a knight in a fair fight. I was frightened that if it were found out, they would burn me, for it is treason for a lady to kill a knight. So I slipped back to my lady’s world, yet…” Her voice trailed off.

“Lady!” exclaimed Ewain. “This is a horrid tale.”

“You are right to be scandalized, for what lady would openly admit such things?” she replied. “But I am putting you on your honor. If you are to learn from me, then you must swear yourself to secrecy.”

“As an honest knight,” Ewain vowed, “I promise that no harm will come to you by any act of mine.”

“Ah, I see I’ve not misjudged you,” said the lady, satisfied, “but I’ve not finished my tale. After that dreadful battle I knew that for me the thought of knighthood was folly. Yet my talent and interest did not die. I watched tournaments and joustings. I saw the mistakes made and watched the ignorant clumsily go about their fighting, no better than

butchers hacking up meat. The good fighters were no accident. Their greatness came from knowing their weapons and shrewdly sizing up their opponents. I watched and learned until I knew more about the art of warring than did any knight upon the field. And there that knowledge sat within me. For a time it festered, turning me bitter and restless. But finally I found that after all there was a way for me.

"Tell me, how many young untried knights have you known who have ridden off, only to return in twelve months' time as sharp as any blade and as sure as any steely spear?"

"I've known some," answered the lad. "Only last year there was Sir Hector. Twelve months ago even I could have bested him, and this season he is back to win the greatest prize at the recent tournament."

The lady laughed softly. "Well, good for him. He was a fine student, one of my best."

"You trained him? He never mentioned you."

"And how could he? What man alive would admit he'd received his lessons from a *woman*?" She turned away from him then and began to walk briskly up the hill.

"Where exactly are we bound, ma'am?" he asked as he hurried his step to keep up.

"To my manor, of course. You know all you need know of me at present. Now it's time to begin your quest for perfect knighthood."

Ewain had come upon the Lady Lochlyn while traveling in a strange wood, to which he had been directed by an older knight, who had sworn that the place sheltered wonders.

It was a wood of oak and pine, tangled and guarded with thick briars. No opening invited entry, so Ewain had had to hack a path with his sword, but at last he found a narrow passage that led to a spring that poured from a mossy mountainside. Above the spring on a fern-covered ridge sat a lady well past middle age, possessing an air of fading beauty. She wore a garland of pale roses twined around her loosely coiled hair. Her clothes were embroidered in gold and silver thread, and a heavy cloak of sturdy wool lay on the ground behind her.

How was it, Ewain wondered in amazement, that such a lady should be sitting out in the wilderness waiting as though she were expecting him?

Ewain followed the Lady Lochlyn to her walled manor house, and there he stayed for twelve long months. He forgot all that had gone before as he lived on meager victuals and wore the rough clothes of a serf while she lessoned him in swordsmanship, marksmanship with bow and arrows, riding, and all the rest. He awoke before light and fell into his bed of straw out in the barn beside his horse well after the moon was up.

"A good horse is better than good armor," she had said on the first day, "and so you will sleep beside yours while I am instructing you. You will comfort and treasure your horse, feed him before you eat, search his wounds before your own. Then, when you have need, you'll have both an instrument and a friend. Remember: A horseman is a single unit, not a man perched on top of a beast."

It was a hard life, she had promised him that. "A knight, like his sword, must be forged by the refining fire," she declared on the second day. "Only through hardship can a man's character be proved."

Day after day, month after month the time sped by, until unbelievably a year had passed. Finally his eye and arm responded without thought or intention; his motion and balance also had become one. At last the lady saw she had the makings of a fighting man.

In the twelfth month, the last month, the Lady Lochlyn seemed more critical than ever before. Her tongue dripped poison and her eyes blazed as she raked him for the slightest error. Then one evening of a day in spring she stopped to regard him. He was dirty and weary from the day's effort. "Well, there it is," she said. "I have done all I can. If you are not ready now, you shall never be."

"Am I a good knight then?" he asked.

"You're nothing until you are tested," she answered, "but you are at least now the fertile ground out of which a good knight might take root. Now get some rest, for tomorrow we shall be off to test the tools that I have made."

The next day he was scrubbed and bathed by servants and given new clothes to wear. She gave him armor, promising him that it was born of magic. "You shall see that it is nearly weightless," she declared. "It has been made so that there is no place where a blade can find a resting place." When he was fitted with a well-crafted sword and shield, she brought out his horse and commanded, "Lead on."

"Where to, ma'am?"

"This is the time when the Lady de Mare holds her spring tournament, and every year she offers a fine prize. Her castle is not a far ride from here. I believe you will find worthy competitors there."

At the castle Ewain and the Lady Lochlyn were each given a splendid chamber, and in the evening there was feasting, tales told, and music played by troubadours. The prize for the winner of the tournament was on display as well: a golden circlet intricately made and worth a great fortune.

Ewain was dazzled by all he saw and equally amazed by his lady. In the great hall she moved with dignity in a silken gown, her striking beauty shining like a flame, her eyes sparkling, and her rosy skin glowing in the candlelight.

On the morning of the tournament, when the ladies took their places on the stand and the competing knights prepared, a parcel was brought to Sir Ewain. Unwrapping it, he found it was the Lady Lochlyn's lavender silk scarf, and he fastened it to the crown of his helmet so that it would float like a pennon when he rode.

The fight was long and glorious, for there were good fighters engaged, and the judges and the ladies in the stands leaned forward, noting the scores. They were expert in the sport and knew the slapdash from good knightly skill. As the day progressed, one single quiet knight met everyone who came against him and unhorsed each, almost effortlessly. When the trumpet called a close to the day, there was no argument. The golden circlet was brought to Ewain. It glittered in his hands. Ewain thanked his hostess and strode to his lady and publicly offered the prize to her. She swept off her headdress, and Ewain placed the circlet upon her head while the company applauded.

Afterward, as they rode away from the castle, the Lady Lochlyn said to him, "I taught you only the use of sword and spear. You must have learned your graceful manners from your mother. With that weapon you will go far."

As they neared the place where they had first met, Ewain said, "Madam, you have given me gifts beyond price. Will you ask something of me?"

"Aye, I shall ask you to remember all I have taught you," she answered quickly.

"That could not be otherwise, my lady," he told her. Then with a note of jealousy he asked, "Will you go back to find another knight?"

"Yes, but I will be critical. It will not be easy to find the likes of you again. Confound it!" she exclaimed with some emotion. "How awful it must be to have a son!"

# A NOTE ABOUT
# CELTIC WARRIORS

*Women warriors are common in the legends of Britain and Ireland,
and the divine patrons of battle were women. The custom of Celtic
women going into battle shocked their Roman enemies. "A whole troop
of foreigners would not be able to withstand a single Celt if he called
his wife to his assistance," wrote the Roman Ammianus Marcellinus
in the fourth century (quote from Nora Chadwick,* The Celts*).*

# MORRIGAN

## FIERCE GODDESS OF WAR

*Morrigan, or Morrigu, figures prominently in Irish sagas.*
*She is the fiercest of the three great war goddesses of Ireland. She*
*can take many different forms, but most often she appears in*
*stories as a black carrion crow presaging death.*

One night, while the great and arrogant warrior Cuchulain was deep in sleep, Morrigan, draped in flowing rainbow-colored robes, stepped soundlessly into his tent. The war goddess smiled down upon the handsome warrior. "Wake up, Cuchulain," she whispered as she rested a delicate hand on his bare shoulder. "I've watched you from afar for a long while. You have great skill and bravery in battle, and for this and your manly beauty, I have come tonight to tell you that I've chosen you to be my mate."

Any other man would have welcomed such words from the beautiful and powerful Morrigan, for to have her favor would ensure a man's lasting success. But not Cuchulain. "You have picked a bad time, madam," he told her. "I am weary from warring, and sleep is all I desire. Tomorrow I must face the battlefield once more."

Surprisingly Morrigan did not grow angry at this rejection. "Tomorrow's battle need not worry you, my beloved. For I will be there by your side to see that you do not fail. So come along and sit awhile with me," she suggested. "Remember, my dear, there is time enough for sleep when you are dead."

But Morrigan's offer of assistance only insulted the proud Cuchulain, and he angrily replied, "A warrior as fine as I has no need of a woman's help."

It was this that brought Morrigan's wrath down on the champion.

In a fury she flew from his tent, vowing he would rue the day that he had made her his enemy.

At dawn the following morning Cuchulain was knocked from his bed by a sudden explosion. Confused by sleep, the warrior struggled to his feet, and without a stitch of clothing or weapons, he ran out of his tent to find the cause. Seeing nothing out of the ordinary about the camp, Cuchulain jumped into his chariot and sped off to search farther.

Unfortunately for Cuchulain, it was not until he was fully awake that he realized the absurdity of his situation. There he was, out in the middle of nowhere, with no notion of where he was heading, without clothes or weapons. Looking about him in embarrassment, he halted his chariot and contemplated his next move.

His humiliation mounted when he suddenly saw a chariot come riding toward him at great speed. As it neared, Cuchulain saw that the rider was a woman with flowing flame-red hair and a blood-red cloak that billowed out behind her as it was caught by the gusty wind. From her regal bearing he knew that it was Morrigan. Cuchulain flushed with shame and anger to think that the goddess should see him like this.

In the next instant the chariot and horse vanished while at the same time Morrigan changed into a great cawing black bird that rose into the sky and streaked away. Long after it had disappeared, its sharp cry still rang in Cuchulain's ears like mocking laughter.

But shaming the arrogant warrior was not enough for Morrigan. Later that morning, on the battlefield where Cuchulain and his troops were fighting, she brought out fifty white heifers harnessed together by a single silver cord. As the cows thundered across the field, the spectacle confused Cuchulain's men and immediately gave the advantage to his enemy.

And still the goddess's vengeance was not satisfied.

Next, Morrigan transformed herself into a long black serpent, and falling upon Cuchulain, she twisted herself around his arms and legs. Just as he was on the verge of freeing himself, Morrigan became a giant she-wolf. Lunging at him, she tore at his arms and legs with razorlike teeth.

All other warfare ceased as the other men looked on, aghast at the frightful struggle. The she-wolf and Cuchulain fought on and on until nightfall. Only then did the goddess retreat, leaving her victim to stagger back to his camp to tend his bloody wounds.

Morrigan had also been badly hurt, and she knew that according to ancient lore, her wounds would not heal unless she could win three blessings from the man who had injured her. Though the very idea that she might succeed in obtaining these from Cuchulain seemed impossible, Morrigan had a plan.

The next day she turned herself into an old hag and went with a milking cow to sit at the side of a crossroad where Cuchulain was sure to pass. There she waited with her pail full of freshly drawn milk, knowing that the warrior would be hot and thirsty by the time he reached her. At last Cuchulain approached, and she called to him, "Here, noble warrior, quench your thirst with a cup of milk."

Gratefully Cuchulain took up the cup and drank, saying, "May the gods bless you, for to be sure, I am thirsty."

When she poured him another, Cuchulain accepted again and once more blessed her for her kindness. And after she had filled and offered him the cup a third time, he gave a third blessing. Morrigan was then thrice blessed, and her wounds were healed.

The man fell back, startled, for just then Morrigan spread sweeping black wings and rose into the sky. The old crone vanished; in her place was a great black crow. Perched upon a tall dead tree, the bird gave no blessing but instead foretold of a swift and grim end to the champion's life.

*Though legend tells that the champion went on to many victories under the protection of Morrigan's rival, the warrior goddess Scathach, at last her vengeful prophecy came to pass, and the superhuman Cuchulain met his death while fighting on the battlefield.*

# GWENDOLEN

### First Warrior Queen
### of Britain

*In his famous* History of the Kings of Britain, *the
twelfth-century writer Geoffrey of Monmouth tells us of the marriage
of Gwendolen and Locrin. The eldest son of Brutus, Locrin inherited
Britain (then called Loegris) in about 1065* B.C., *and his two
younger brothers ruled Wales and Scotland, respectively.*

The high king of Britain was Locrin, a man without equal
throughout the Mighty Isle for manly beauty. Locrin remained
unmarried, for he had no want of adoring maidens to keep
him entertained. But his people expected him to wed and to produce
many heirs. "A king without an heir is half a king," they declared. So
the elders went to Locrin and persuaded him that it was time that he
chose a wife.

"Indeed, there are many fair maidens. Pray, how should I choose?"
asked the king.

"Is there no one among them that you could love?" they asked
in turn.

"No," said Locrin with a broad smile, "for all of them please me.
But come, my good advisers. Is there one *you* would have me choose
over the rest? Let us hear of it now."

"Gwendolen, daughter of Corineus, high king of Cornwall," they
answered. "There is not another more fitting in all the land, and there
is no one prettier, lord."

"Then I must go see the maiden." Thus Locrin journeyed to
Cornwall, and there in summer he met Gwendolen for the first time.
His advisers had not lied. She was indeed a beauty: Her hair was red as

copper, her eyes were greener than the sea, and her skin was like the lilies blooming in the summer sun. Locrin saw that she was also as proud as she was beautiful, though it did not keep him from asking to wed her.

Corineus was pleased to join his daughter with Locrin in marriage, and a date was set. Now, the custom in those days was to perform a ceremony in the same half of the year in which it was proposed, else bad luck was believed to follow. So since the couple were betrothed in midsummer, they agreed to be wed before Samhain (autumn).

In the meantime Locrin was called back home to fight an enemy's army that threatened his lands. Many lives were lost while the battle waged on long after all the summer blooms had faded.

Corineus consulted with his daughter. "It is a bad omen, my girl. Another time must be set for your wedding."

If Gwendolen was troubled, she did not show it, and she said, "It is not fitting to talk of weddings when there is a war to be won, Father."

At last Locrin defeated the invaders, and the spoils of war were divided. Locrin took gold and treasure as his rightful share and was also given the group of slaves who had been held captive on the enemy's ship. Among them was a woman so exquisite that when Locrin saw her, it seemed his heart stood still. He was told that her name was Estrildis and that she had been stolen from her homeland in far-off Germany. Surely there can be no other as lovely, as perfect in all the world, he thought, for her skin is as luminous as a pearl and her hair as golden as wheat ripening under the shimmering sun.

When Locrin addressed her, the delicate and gentle girl buried her lovely face in her slender hands and wept softly. Locrin's heart melted. If he had been asked to choose from among all the treasures before him, he would have gladly cast them all aside and taken this one solitary girl for his own.

From that moment onward Estrildis was seldom far from Locrin's side, and his love for the girl only grew until it filled him to overflowing. He decided that he must make her his queen. But when word of his decision spread, his people were opposed. "The high king should not have a foreigner and a slave for his queen," they insisted.

So Locrin locked Estrildis away in a hidden sanctuary where she would be safe. There he created a splendid paradise with fragrant plants and lush fruit trees. In secret then he visited her, while he took Gwendolen to be his bride and queen to please his people and her powerful father, whom he had no wish to make his enemy.

When Gwendolen arrived in Locrin's kingdom, she turned watchful, jealous eyes everywhere, for she had heard the gossip. But she uncovered no evidence to prove that Locrin was untrue, for he was a dutiful, devoted husband. And so she came to believe, along with everyone else, that he had sent the other away.

Years passed, and secretly Locrin continued to visit his true love. Estrildis gave him a daughter while Gwendolen gave him a son. Then the time came when Corineus died. Great was Gwendolen's grief at the loss of her father, and Locrin too sincerely grieved for his friend, but a fear was lifted from him as well. At last he could make his beloved Estrildis his queen, for now that the mighty Corineus was gone he need no longer fear reprisal.

When the period of mourning was over, Locrin summoned the elders and said, "I am going to send Gwendolen away, and in her place I shall make Estrildis my queen." This time when they begged him to reconsider, he refused.

When Gwendolen heard, she searched her reflection in the mirror and asked, "Am I no longer beautiful?" It was not so; she was as lovely as ever. But when a man's heart is truly with another, there is nothing that can win him away.

Adorned in her finest robes and jewels, Gwendolen strode into the king's great hall to confront her husband. Her eyes flashed as she asked, "What is this plan of yours, Husband? When we took our vows, you did not say then to me or my father that this marriage was temporary. Have I not been a loving wife and given you a son and heir who makes us both proud?"

Locrin saw her regal bearing and her iron will, and his thoughts

went to Estrildis and her soft voice and gentle touch. There was nothing Gwendolen could say or do that would win him to her, and at that moment she saw the truth of it in his eyes.

Frustrated, she fought back the hot tears that threatened to well up in her eyes and shouted, "Answer me, Husband! I am your queen and of royal blood now and before you wed me. Would you cast me aside for a slave?"

Locrin was silent for a long time. At last he answered heavily, "Aye, I would, lady," before he turned away from her.

Now vengeance filled Gwendolen's mind and heart. In an icy voice she replied, "So you believe that since my father is dead, there is no one to stop you from doing whatever you wish. Well, by the gods," she cried, "you will find that there is!"

That day she gave orders to collect her belongings. Then, summoning her warriors and chariots, she set out that very night for Cornwall, leaving nothing of hers behind.

Without thought to the consequences Locrin brought forth Estrildis and had her crowned his queen.

When Gwendolen arrived in Cornwall, her kinswomen wept for her, but she told them, "Shed no tears for me. My curse is on Locrin, and he will pay."

Then she ordered craftsmen to fashion weapons and chariots. She chose the finest warhorses, claiming four of the best for her own. Arming her warriors, she took for herself helmet and shield, long spears and short swift spears, long swords and a dagger that never missed its mark; all were bejeweled and inlaid with gold.

Then she called the mighty men of Cornwall to her, and in a fortnight, armed and ready, Gwendolen and her army attacked Locrin's domain. Wherever they went they ravaged the land. The bards sang of Gwendolen's triumph, and Locrin's advisers pleaded with him, "Lord, be quick! Remember, you are high king of all England. Go against her before it is too late."

"How can I? She has been my wife, and her son is mine also," he told them.

"None of that matters now, lord," they insisted. "If you do not act, all the country will be destroyed. As king you have the sovereign duty to protect it."

So with a heavy heart Locrin summoned his royal war band and went to meet the force of Gwendolen. Between Stour and the river the armies with thundering hooves and sharpened swords met and clashed, and soon the green earth ran red with the blood. At last Locrin came face-to-face with Gwendolen and said, "Lady, it was a dark day when you chose to go against the high king of all England."

"Indeed it was, lord," answered Gwendolen scornfully. "'Twas a darker one when you cast me aside for another." Then she raised her voice so that all could hear: "It sickens me to see my warriors die for such a cause as this. The quarrel is between the high king and the queen of Cornwall. Therefore, let the armies put down their weapons while he and I meet in single combat."

Locrin sighed and said, "Very well, lady. If that be your wish." But his heart was stricken at the thought of fighting Gwendolen.

Both armies fell silent as the king and queen, long swords in one hand, daggers in the other, clashed. Gwendolen was filled with fury, but Locrin, the mighty warrior, today had no will in him to fight this fight. Quickly he was overcome, and in one swift stroke she drove her dagger into his heart. Then, with her long sword, Gwendolen cut his head from his body and raised it for all to see. With tears in her eyes, she drew Locrin's handsome face to hers and kissed those lips one last time. "For beauty, Husband, you had no equal. Gladly I have known no man's lips but yours. If not for the wrong you did me, nothing on this earth would have parted us."

The others wept as they watched her tie the head by its long black locks to her chariot. He had been a great king, they all thought, but not one among them blamed Gwendolen. Her captain came forward after a moment and said, "Now, my lady, is the matter done?"

"Not yet," Gwendolen answered. "There is still one last thing to attend to." Then she had Estrildis and her daughter summoned.

When Gwendolen saw Estrildis for the first time, a still greater anger filled her. "For this pale creature, Locrin threw me away! My curse on you both."

Estrildis covered her face and sobbed at the sight of her beloved Locrin's head fastened to the queen's chariot and said not a word.

Then Gwendolen looked upon Severn, Estrildis and Locrin's daughter. The onlookers were struck by the maiden's great unearthly beauty, for she was even more exquisite than her mother. Not one among them could have willingly raised a hand against the girl. But Gwendolen, powered by her hurt and vengeance, commanded that both mother and daughter be drowned in the river that ran along the battlefield. Only then did Estrildis speak out, begging that her daughter be spared. But the queen closed her ears to such pleas, saying, "I concede only that from this day hence the great river shall be called

Severn in her honor." Then she ordered that they both be cast into the water, and thus the deed was done as she herself watched.

Estrildis died almost willingly, for with Locrin gone she had no wish to live. As for the young innocent maiden who had no blame in this affair, the shining spirits that live beneath the waters took pity upon her. They brought her to their own crystal world where none grows old or sad. There she did not die but dwells in bliss as the guardian spirit of Severn, the great river that bears her name.

Gwendolen took Locrin's place and reigned as high queen of all the land until her son reached maturity. Then she gave up that throne and returned to Cornwall to rule until her death. Those who knew her said she never loved again.

# BOADICEA

## The Woman with the Sword

*During the Roman Empire, a number of foreign
queens fought against the Roman rule, including Cleopatra,
who sat on the throne of Egypt, and Queen Candace, who ruled the
neighboring kingdom of Ethiopia. And then there was Boadicea. Her
name came to mean "Woman with the Sword," for she raised an army
of 230,000 British men and women to defy the mighty power of Rome.
Through her mother's royal lineage she claimed descent from the kings of
Troy and the Ptolemys of Egypt. Her marriage to Arviragus made her
queen of the Iceni, who lived in Essex, Norfolk, and Cambridgeshire—
today known as East Anglia in England. This is her story.*

At the age of forty Boadicea was at the height of her beauty
and the mother of two grown daughters, Tasca and Camorra.
She was tall and striking, with penetrating green eyes and
long red hair. Riding her chariot into battle, she wore a heavy gold torc
around her neck, and a mantle fastened with a brooch covered a tunic
of many colors. Such a courageous warrior queen was beloved by her
people. She inspired them with a passion to reclaim their liberty, and
they took up arms against the Romans who had dominated and en-
slaved them for seventeen long years.

It was the first century A.D., and Nero was emperor of Rome.
Greatly despised, Nero was cruel and greedy, but above all, he was
completely mad. Boadicea and her husband had an uneasy truce with
the emperor. For eleven years Nero permitted them to rule their
wealthy Iceni nation, but they had to pay a heavy yearly tax in gold for
the privilege. Then, in A.D. 61, Boadicea's husband suddenly died.

Without warning the Roman army invaded. It seized the Iceni monarch's property and imprisoned his relations. Heavy taxes were imposed on all, including the already overburdened poor. When Boadicea was unable to pay the large sums Nero demanded, she was dragged out into the street and whipped, and her daughters were violated. Now destitute, Boadicea was burning for revenge.

Her flesh still stinging from the bloody flogging, Boadicea went before her people. "We already know the difference between our ancient way of life and foreign despotism," she declared. "Isn't freedom better than slavery whatever the cost? If there is any hope of leaving the gift of liberty to our children, now is the time to fight. The Romans are rabbits trying to rule over wolves. See how they'll run from us when we show them our teeth!" Then she raised her mantle and released a hare she had concealed. Terrified, the animal ran off, hotly pursued by a pack of Boadicea's hounds.

Amid cheers from the crowd, Boadicea called down the blessings of the bountiful goddess Andraste and summoned her people to act. The Iceni were more than ready for revolt, and soon Boadicea and her forces were joined by patriots from all parts of the island.

The Romans, though ignorant of the impending rebellion, saw dismal omens of doom. One day a statue of the winged Roman goddess Victory suddenly turned its back on its worshipers and, tumbling from its pedestal, fell to pieces. Then the sea turned blood-red, and impressions of dead horses and human bodies were left by the receding tide. The Romans shuddered with fear, but nothing had prepared them for what was to follow.

In the dead of night Boadicea's army rushed down upon the nearby Roman colonies, putting to death all who opposed them. Battle after battle followed, and with each conquest Boadicea and her army grew bolder. At last they marched on London and captured the city.

After this the Roman generals were too terrified to venture into battle against the victorious queen whose warriors vastly outnumbered theirs. But in time the Roman governor decided on a plan. Carefully he chose a narrow valley to attack the Britons, a place where Boadicea's army could not make good use of its superior numbers. Indeed, only as many troops as could fit into the valley at any one time could engage the Romans' smaller number.

The morning before the battle Boadicea rode her chariot around her forces with both Tasca and Camorra by her side. "Remember, my beloved Britons," she called out, encouraging her warriors, "our fight today sends a message to the Roman tyrant who has tried to make us his slaves. None of us will ever rest until every Briton can throw off the chains of slavery and again embrace liberty."

But the victory of that decisive battle went to the Romans, and eager to avenge their past defeats, they slaughtered the Britons indiscriminately. Though Boadicea's army was decimated, she and her daughters miraculously escaped the carnage.

Roman historians tell us that Boadicea took poison—a gesture of purest disdain for her enemy, whom she despised, for suicide among the Celtic nobility was the only answer to defeat.

Although immediate retribution for the rebellion was swift and cruel, the Britons refused to give in and resume life as it had been. Tasca, Boadicea's daughter, adopted her mother's name and continued the fight. In time the Romans grew weary of the relentless Britons, for they saw that the stubborn rebels would no longer be intimidated by force. Finally a new Roman rule instituted a policy of appeasement that improved conditions for all Britain. So Boadicea did not die in vain.

*Yet there were those who swore that the beloved queen was deathless. Mysteriously her body was never found, and legends sprang up concerning the great queen. Many declared that Boadicea was a Celtic warrior goddess come to earth in the guise of a mortal solely to take up Britain's cause.*

*Today no one knows the whereabouts of the heroic queen's grave. Stonehenge was once claimed as her monument. Her ghost, it is said, haunts Epping Forest, and in 1950 she was seen driving her chariot out of the mist near Cammeringham in Lincolnshire.*

*Epping Forest is not far from the queen's last battle. Perhaps she dwells there still between dark forest and wild heartland, moving regally through her tall timbered palace, as great and bounteous a figure as ever she was in life.*

# MELLA

### YOUNG FRIEND OF
### THE PYTHON

*This tale of young Mella's courage and later her
role as tribal leader is based upon the oral history of the
Buhera Ba Rowzi tribe from Zimbabwe.*

In a home of reeds and fiber on the edge of the lush green forest, Mella sat upon a grass mat and held her ailing father's frail hand. He had once been the wise, strong leader of the tribe, but now he could barely lift his head. The family had offered prayers and many sacrifices for his recovery. The tribal healers tried to use their magic. They played music from their pipes and drums, but they could not rouse him. Day by day his condition worsened, and as he grew weaker, the family began to prepare for his death. All, that is, except Mella.

One night while the villagers were sleeping, Mella walked out into the forest, following the footpath to a clearing. The moon overhead shone like a golden crescent in the black velvet sky. All along the moonlight had been her guide. Now she stopped and looked up at Bomu Rambi, the merciful moon goddess.

Mella called out, "Please, Bomu Rambi, give me some sign to show what I must do to save my father."

Suddenly the wind swept through the trees, and the branches gently swayed with the mysterious presence of the goddess. All at once Mella heard the soft words of Bomu Rambi floating toward her on the wind. "You must go to the Python Healer," said the moon goddess.

Though the night was warm, Mella shivered. The Python Healer struck terror into the villagers' hearts. His cave stood at the foot of a mountain in the deepest, thickest part of the jungle, and no one dared go there. Some time ago Mella's own brothers had sought him out for their father's sake. But they had fled in horror from the entrance of the python's cave, and returned to the village so terrified that they could not speak of what they had seen.

Mella returned home, but she could not sleep. That night she made up her mind to do as the moon goddess had advised, regardless of the risk. At dawn she rose before everyone else. Quickly she gathered a few things for her journey and set out.

She traveled day and night, passing ferns higher than her head, climbing rocky hills, crossing streams, sleeping in the open. Through it all, her thoughts were only of her father, and they gave her courage to go on.

At last, with the moon just a faint sliver in the sky, Mella came upon the entrance to the cave of the Python Healer. She sucked in her breath and stopped. For the first time fear took hold. Fighting back the wish to run, the young girl struggled to steady her voice as she called out, "Python Healer, the merciful Bomu Rambi has sent me. My name is Mella, and I come to ask for your healing power to cure my father, who is gravely ill."

The jungle fell silent. Even the birds and the crickets were still as Mella waited with only the sound of her pounding heart to listen to. Then two emerald eyes shone from the darkness of the cave, and a voice thundered out, "How is it that the bravest of your village flee from me, yet one small girl comes asking for favors? Child, are you too young to realize that I could crush you with my strangling coils?"

Mella swallowed, trying to steady her trembling. She raised her head and gazed back at the huge shadowy silhouette with its burning eyes. "I fear you, mighty healer. But I have nowhere else to go. I prayed to Bomu Rambi, and she told me to seek your help."

"Your love for your father gives you courage, little one. But are you brave enough to do what is necessary? Will you let me coil myself around you?"

Though she knew that she was making herself easy prey for the serpent, Mella quickly agreed. "If this is what you ask in return for healing my father, I will not refuse."

At the same moment the clouds gathered overhead and covered the pale light of the moon. All was blackest night as the giant python slithered out of the cave. Mella could see nothing as the sound of the serpent's hissing drew closer and closer until she could feel his breath upon her face. Slowly he rose and began to wind himself around and around her. At last only Mella's head, arms, and legs were free of the python's coils. In a hissing whisper the Python Healer told Mella to return with him to her home.

The serpent's weight was heavy, yet Mella struggled onward, following the path with her head held high. It was nightfall when they finally reached the village. When the villagers saw the monster, they ran for their weapons. But Mella called out to them, "Stop, do not harm us! You have nothing to fear. It is Mella! I have carried the Python Healer here to help my father."

Once beside the sick man, the Python Healer uncoiled, telling Mella to take healing bark and muchonga oil from the medicine pouch he kept hung around his neck. He instructed her to make a fire with them, and soon the vapors filled the room, giving off a sweet, smoky scent. The Python Healer began to chant, and slowly both Mella and her father fell into a restful trance.

Time passed—minutes, hours, it was impossible to say. Then the ailing man moved slowly to sit up. After a few moments longer he was on his feet. Mella could hardly believe her eyes; so many months had passed with her father scarcely able to lift his head.

"It is a miracle," cried Mella's father as he embraced his daughter. And turning to the Python Healer, he said, "Please stay with us so that I may prepare a grand celebration in your honor."

The serpent made no reply as he silently began to wrap himself around Mella once more. The young girl understood, and having said farewell to her father, she set out once more to bring the Python Healer back to his home.

When they arrived, he said, "Come into my cave."

Mella was past fear after all she had been through, and though she did not relish the idea of seeing the broken remains of victims the python had devoured, she followed him. As she went into the cave, her eyes widened with surprise at a glimmering light ahead. A few steps farther, and she saw that this light came from a mountain of shimmering golden treasure. There were baskets and baskets overflowing with gold and jewels of every color.

"You may take whatever you like," said the Python Healer, "for your courage should be rewarded."

Mella shook her head and said, "It is you who should be rewarded for healing my father."

"All the same you will take something," the python said. When Mella made no move to do so, the python said, "Here, then, I will choose for you."

Then he went to a large basket, and after a few moments he drew out a beautiful gold necklace from which hung an amulet of heavy gold cut in the shape of the crescent moon. Giving it to her, the serpent said, "You shall have the symbol of the moon goddess to remember me by. Take it, child, as a token of my friendship."

When the people of the village heard what had happened, envy entered the hearts of three men. They began to plot to kill the python so that they could steal his treasure. By chance Mella overheard them scheming. Quickly she took her bow and arrows and ran back to the Python Healer's cave, ready to give her life if necessary to save her friend. When the men arrived in the dead of night, they were met by the serpent and Mella. All at once thunder rolled, fire burst forth from the Python Healer's magic charms, and the men fell down dead in fright.

In the years that followed, Mella lived with her father in great happiness. And when, at last after a long full life, Mella's father died, her people made her leader of their tribe, for no one was more courageous or more loving than she.

# YAKAMI

SLAYER OF THE
SEA MONSTER

*The Japanese heroine Yakami is also the name
of the divine princess mentioned in other* Kojiki *tales
from the island of Kyushu. Ancient Chinese legend
has the heroine Li Chi in a similar tale.*

Along the coastline of Kyushu where the waters of the Pacific flow, there Yakami once lived. For as long as the young girl could remember, she had spent her days diving for pearls in the inlets along the shore. It was a happy life. She and her friends worked side by side and shouted with joy each time an oyster was opened to reveal a perfect pearl.

But all this came to an abrupt end when Yakami's parents were arrested and sent to prison for speaking against those in power. Yakami was shattered. The day her parents were taken away, Yakami's friends gathered around her, but there was little anyone could do or say to soften the pain of her loss. Many in the village would have taken her in, but as time passed, the young girl felt she could no longer remain. Her sole wish was to find her parents, and she had a plan.

She went to the docks, looking for one of the fishermen to hire her. "On the island of Tenega," the child told the first fisherman she met, "my parents are being kept prisoner. If you will take me there, I promise to work on your fishing boat without pay."

The fisherman looked at her sadly, and shaking his head, he replied, "I would like to help, but my own family might suffer if I did. Give up this wild notion, child, for no one will be fool enough to take you, and you can never succeed."

Indeed the fisherman spoke the truth, for when the others working along the dock learned what the child wanted, they all turned away from her. Finally Yakami decided to take matters into her own hands. When it grew dark that moonless night, she went back to the dock and slipped into one of the small fishing boats. With only the stars looking down on her, she rowed out, full of hope that she would soon see her parents again.

After days and nights of rowing she finally reached the island. But when she asked for news of her parents, people were too fearful even to discuss the matter. Anxiously Yakami looked around, not knowing where to turn next, and saw in the distance a small cedarwood shrine perched upon a cliff. Though she was weary from her long journey, she suddenly thought that if she could reach the shrine, all would work out for her, and so she began to climb the cliff.

When she arrived at the top, Yakami saw that on the far side there was a sheer drop to the sea below. The sea breezes were cool, and around the shrine were fragrant flowers. Comforted by all this, she heaved a sigh of relief, sat down to rest against a shade tree, and closed her eyes.

She must have fallen asleep, for when she opened her eyes, Yakami saw a priest in dark robes beside a sobbing young girl dressed in white. Unaware of Yakami's presence, they stood dangerously close to the edge of the cliff, their backs turned away from her as they gazed down at the sea. Then, to Yakami's horror, the priest made a move to push the girl off the cliff. Yakami cried out, causing the priest to stop and look back at her.

"Child, please do not interfere," the priest said to Yakami. "This girl has been chosen to be sacrificed to the dragon living beneath the sea. Long ago the people on the island made a bargain with the monster. So long as once a year on this day we cast a young girl into the sea, the dragon is appeased and will not destroy everyone living here."

"Let her go," said Yakami. "I will take her place. I am all alone; I have nothing—no family any longer, no home to call my own." The next moment, before the priest could reply, to his and the other girl's astonishment Yakami dived off the cliff and plunged into the water.

She was no stranger to the ocean; indeed it was like a second home to her. All her years of diving for pearls had made her a powerful swimmer, and her lungs were used to the deep waters. Yakami let herself drop down, down, down to the very depths of the sea. As she reached the sandy floor, she drew out her hunting dagger and clenched it between her teeth.

"If the dragon wants to devour me," she told herself, "he will have to fight me first."

The next second Yakami saw a magnificent crystal palace with towering coral pillars. From within, two eyes burning like fire stared at her. There, coiled and ready, was the monstrous dragon. It sprang out, but its enormous scaly hulk was not as quick as the agile Yakami, and she easily escaped the first attack. Old and unused to fighting, the dragon shook its ugly head in surprise and struck out at her again. But Yakami swam above the dragon's head, and then, with her dagger poised, she came down to stab it in the neck.

Over and over she drove in the dagger until dark green blood flowed from the wounds,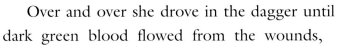

turning the water almost black. Blinded by the darkness, unable to find its tiny adversary, the dragon whirled around and around. Swiftly taking the advantage, Yakami struck again and again, this time driving the dagger into the dragon's heart. It all happened so very quickly, and in a few brief moments the dragon fell dead before her.

At the surface the priest and the young girl had watched intently as the water turned almost black, and then—to their utter amazement—there was Yakami.

The news of Yakami's triumph spread quickly throughout the islands. Soon there was not a person who was not talking of the remarkable girl who had boldly conquered the deadly dragon and in so doing won them all freedom from its evil power. Indeed the news even reached those officials in charge of the prison where Yakami's parents were held. As a reward for her great bravery, a decree was signed releasing both her parents so that they could be reunited with their child. Together at last, they were never again to be parted until the end of their days.

*Long after she was gone from the island, the famous tale of Yakami's courage was often told. The tiny cedarwood shrine on top of the cliff had her name carved on it for all to see, and year after year the islanders gathered on the anniversary of that day to celebrate the girl they called the Selfless One, the Courageous One, who had done so much for the people of the island.*

# A NOTE ABOUT NATIVE AMERICAN WARRIORS

*Warfare for many Native American tribes was considered an exciting, though dangerous, sport. In fact, on the battlefield Native American warriors were not unlike medieval knights at a tournament, for in both cases their honor, courage, and skill were tested.*

*In many tribes, untried youth earned the eagle feather, a symbol of coming of age, through success on the battlefield. Killing was not necessary to gain honor, however. The custom of counting coup (pronounced KOO) was an opportunity to best one's opponent without taking a life. The warrior, using a curved couping stick, lightly tapped his or her opponent while in combat. The tap was not fatal, but it did gain honor for the warrior and disgrace for the recipient. Of course warriors also killed in such contests, but killing was not the goal in warfare. To bring death to an entire tribe was unthinkable and achieved only dishonor for the victors. At the same time, if too many of one's own warriors were lost in battle, even if the outcome resulted in victory, a leader lost the respect of the group.*

*Leaders attracted followers with their valor and "good medicine" (personal power). The leader did not actually command or demand obedience; what kept a war party loyal was the leader's prestige and charisma. Otherwise, the warriors followed their own codes, for a war party was not regimented as were armies of the European colonists.*

# WINYAN OHITIKA

## BRAVE WOMAN OF THE SIOUX

*The Hunkpapa are a part of the Lakota Sioux, who comprise the Seven Tribes, or Ocheti Shakowin (Seven Campfires). They are the hard-riding Red Knights of the Prairie, and theirs was the nomadic culture of the tepee, the dog, and later the horse. They pray with the sacred pipe and go on sacred vision quests. Originally friendly to the white settlers, the Lakota were finally forced to fight to defend their ancient hunting ground. The Lakota warriors fought their last battle, against impossible odds, at Wounded Knee in 1890.*

More than a hundred years ago a Sioux Indian tribe called the Hunkpapa lived at Spirit Lake in the land that is now called Minnesota. Their chief, Tawa Makoce, had once been an unbeatable warrior, and in old age he was revered for his great wisdom. The chief had three sons and one daughter. The sons tried to live up to their father's reputation, but it was no easy task to match the deeds of such a noble hero. One by one they recklessly fought the Sioux's lifelong enemy, the Crow. The young men were brave and fought well, but in the end one after the other they all were killed in battle. Now only the daughter remained. She was proud and beautiful, and in those days she was called Makhta.

Many a chief's son wished to wed Makhta. One of them was a strong warrior named Red Horn, who asked many times for her. But Makhta refused all marriage proposals, saying, "I will not take a husband until I have avenged the death of my three brothers."

Another young man, Little Eagle, wished to marry her as well. But he was not the son of a chief. He was shy and poor and had not distinguished himself on the battlefield. Though he watched Makhta from afar and loved her deeply, Little Eagle knew all too well that he had little chance of winning the chief's daughter.

In those days the Crow Nation wished to lay claim to the banks of the upper Missouri, an area the Sioux occupied and called their own. When the Crow mounted an attack, the Sioux assembled a mighty war party to face their enemy and try to force them back. Red Horn and Little Eagle were among them. Makhta dressed in her best clothes and, wearing a necklace of beautiful shells, went to join them. "I will ride with you," said the girl. When they refused her offer, Makhta went to the old chief. "Father," said she, "in the name of my dead brothers I must go fight with the others. Do not prevent me."

The old chief's eyes filled with tears of sorrow, but he felt pride at her brave words. "Now you are all I have. I fear I shall lose you too, as I have lost my other children. Yet I know that your mind is made up. How you remind me of myself," he said. "I will not stop you. Take my warbonnet, and go into battle with my blessing."

Makhta took her brothers' weapons and her father's best horse and warbonnet and rode out with the warriors. The war party found that the Crow people's number far exceeded their own, but they bravely advanced. With the fearless Makhta riding alongside them, what warrior could think of retreat?

As they proceeded, she gave her eldest brother's lance and shield to Red Horn. "Count coup in my eldest brother's name," she called to him. To Little Eagle she gave her second brother's bow and arrows. "Count coup for my middle brother," she said. For herself she kept her youngest brother's war club and her father's old couping stick.

When the fighting began, Makhta hung back and made the Sioux's shrill war cry to urge the warriors on by singing bravehearted songs. But when she saw that they were losing the battle, she joined the fighting.

Now Makhta chose not to kill her enemy. Risking her life time and again, she used her father's couping stick, and in the old Sioux tradition she boldly rode up and tapped one Crow warrior after another. In so doing, she brought down upon them utter disgrace but not death.

The sight of Makhta challenging the Crow made the Sioux feel stronger, and they fought all the harder against the crushing odds.

Nonetheless, the Crow's numbers were too great, and they continued to advance. Then Makhta's horse was wounded, and she fell to the ground amid the fighting, defenseless. Red Horn rode by and saw her distress, but she was too proud to call out to him for help, and he passed her. Then Little Eagle came riding toward her. He dismounted and gave her his horse. Makhta mounted and called to him, expecting him to join her. But he refused, saying, "This horse is too weary from fighting to carry us both." Before she could insist, he struck the horse's rump, causing it to bolt, as he had intended. Then he turned and continued to fight on the ground. It was the last she saw him, for in no time the Crow brought him down.

As the hours of fighting passed, the Crow began to fall behind. This was the chance Makhta had hoped for. Calling out a wild war cry, she rallied the Sioux behind her. Now, with the forces gathered together, they mounted a fresh attack. Inch by inch they pushed the Crow back until they drove them off their lands and won the battle.

This was a decisive battle, for the Crow Nation never again returned to try to invade Missouri territory. Yet such a great victory cost many lives. Among the fallen was the brave warrior Little Eagle, who gave up his horse and his life to save Makhta. But Red Horn survived, and the Sioux broke his bow, scorning him for failing to aid her.

Then they raised Little Eagle's body onto a tall scaffolding. There they laid him to rest with many prayers, knowing that he would be welcomed into the Spirit World as a great warrior. In mourning for Little Eagle, Makhta tore her dress and cut off her hair, and asked that she be treated as his widow as long as she lived.

The Sioux renamed Makhta Winyan Ohitika, meaning "brave woman."

# ALIQUIPISO
## THE GIRL WHO
## SAVED HER TRIBE

*Though today no specific Native American nation claims
this courageous heroine as its own, in the early 1900s the story
of her selfless bravery was attributed to the oral tradition of the
Oneida people. The Oneida, the People of the Rock, originally lived
near Oneida Lake in New York, and they are one of the original
Five Nations of the Iroquois League. Interestingly, like the Celts, the
Oneida trace their descent through the mother, and the longhouses
they lived in were owned by the women of the nation.*

Long before the colonists settled in the New World, a tribe called the Mingoes threatened Aliquipiso's people. Over and over the Mingoes attacked her people's villages, killing men and boys in battle and kidnapping the womenfolk. At last the villages lay deserted, their homes burned to ashes, and the fields were fallow.

The survivors fled into the forest and took shelter in a remote mountain cave. The Mingoes went searching, but they could not find them. For a time the survivors were safe, but if they left their shelter to search for food, they risked being caught and killed.

The remaining warrior chiefs and elders of the tribe met in council to decide what must be done. But time passed, and no one could think of a solution. Then Aliquipiso, a girl barely eleven years old, came forward. "Last night," she said, "the good spirits sent me a dream that has shown me a way to save our people."

The group of men looked at Aliquipiso doubtfully. How could this girl help? they wondered. The eldest chief asked her to explain. "In my dream I was given to see that above where we are hiding there are

hundreds of giant boulders and rocks," said the girl. "When the time is right, our warriors must stand ready to throw these rocks down upon the Mingoes."

"That is all very well, child, but how will we get our enemy to that spot?" asked the old chief.

"I will let the Mingoes capture me, and when they demand that I reveal our hiding place, I will lead them to the place where high above them our warriors will be waiting to crush them."

The council listened to the girl's plan in amazement. "Truly the Great Spirit speaks through you," observed the old chief, "but, Aliquipiso, do you understand that this brave deed will mean your death?"

"Like any brave warrior, I am not afraid to give my life for my people," the girl replied.

"We, your grateful people, will not forget your courage," said the old chief, and the entire council agreed.

That night all alone the girl climbed down the steep mountain cliff to the forest below. In the early morning the Mingo scouts found her wandering in the wood as if she were lost. When they brought her before their chief, he commanded, "Show us the way to where your people are hiding. If you do, we will adopt you into our tribe. But if you refuse, you will be tortured until death will seem like a mercy from your suffering."

Knowing that they would doubt her if she gave in too easily, Aliquipiso vowed, "I will never tell you."

So the Mingoes tied Aliquipiso to a post and burned her with fire. By nightfall even her torturers were awed by her endurance and courage. At last Aliquipiso pretended to weaken. "Please," she cried, "I can stand no more pain. I will tell you everything, only do not hurt me anymore."

Then the Mingoes took her from the post and tied her hands behind her back. Pushing her ahead of them, they warned, "Do not try to break free, or we will kill you."

Aliquipiso led the way while the rest of the war party soundlessly crept forward. Under cover of night they moved, following the young girl through pine groves and on hidden deer paths, along streambeds and swamps.

At dawn Aliquipiso came to a halt beneath a high cliff of sheer rock. "Closer, come closer," whispered the girl to the others. The Mingoes gathered around her. "Thinking themselves safe," she whispered, "my people are sleeping above us." Then, pointing to a spot on the side of the cliff, she said, "Here, look! This is the secret path that will lead you straight up the mountain to them."

Now with the Mingoes crowded around her in a tight circle, suddenly Aliquipiso cried out in a piercing voice, "The enemy has come!"

The Mingoes hardly had time to cut her down before the rocks came raining down upon them, crushing everyone. So many died there that morning that the rest of the invading band gave up tormenting her people and finally retreated to their own lands. Indeed, thanks to Aliquipiso's courage, the Mingoes never made war on her people again.

*Thereafter, her story was told and retold wherever her people gathered around their campfires to speak of their history. Generation after generation know the story of the gentle girl whose sacrifice and bravery saved her tribe. And the holders of their history say that when Aliquipiso gave her life that day, the Great Spirit changed her hair into woodbine vines, believed to be good medicine by her people. From her fallen body, they go on to say, honeysuckle bloomed, and among her people even today this flower is called the blood of brave woman in loving memory of her.*

# SELECTED BIBLIOGRAPHY

AFRICAN

Arnott, K. *African Myths and Legends Retold*. London: Oxford University Press, 1962.

Itayemi, P., and P. Gurrey. *Folktales and Fables*. New York: Penguin, 1953.


AMAZONIAN

Salmonson, Jessica A. *The Encyclopedia of Amazons*. New York: Paragon House, 1991.

Tyrrell, Blake William. *Amazons: A Study in Athenian Mythmaking*. New York: Johns Hopkins University Press, 1984.


BRITISH

Ashe, Geoffrey. *Mythology of the British Isles*. London: Methuen, 1990.

Dumezil, George. *Archaic Roman Religion*, vol. 1. Chicago: University of Chicago Press, 1970.

Spence, Lewis. *Boadicea, Warrior Queen of the Britons*. London: Robert Hale.


CELTIC

Campbell, J. F. *Popular Tales of the West Highlands* (1860). Aldershot, U.K.: Wildwood House, 1983.

Chadwick, Nora. *The Celts*. New York: Penguin, 1970.

———. *The Druids*. Cardiff, U.K.: Cardiff University Press, 1966.

MacCulloch, J. C. *Celtic Mythology*, vol. 3, *Mythology of All Races*, ed. Louis Herbert Gray. New York: Cooper Square Publishers, 1964.

Markale, Jean. *Women of the Celts*. Rochester, Vt.: Inner Traditions International, 1986.


GENERAL

Bell, Robert E. *Women of Classical Mythology—A Biographical Dictionary*. Santa Barbara, Calif.: ABC-CLIO USA, 1991.

Bonnefoy, Yves. *Mythologies: A Dictionary*, vol. 1. Chicago: University of Chicago Press, 1991.

Clayton, Ellen. *Female Warriors*, vol. 1. London: Tinsley Brothers, 1879.

Gaster, Theodor H. *The Oldest Stories in the World*. New York: Viking, 1952.

Guirand, Felix, ed. *New Larousse Encyclopedia of Mythology*. London: Larousse, 1960.

Landon, Stephan H. *Semitic Mythology*, vol. 5, *Mythology of All Races*, ed. by J.C. MacCulloch. New York: Cooper Square Publishers, 1964.

Monaghan, Patricia. *The Book of Goddesses and Heroines*. St. Paul, Minn.: Llewellyn Publications, 1990.

Newark, Tim. *Women Warlords: An Illustrated Military History of Ancient and Medieval Female Warriors.* London: Blandford, 1989.

Simek, Rudolf. *Dictionary of Northern Mythology.* Suffolk, U.K.: St. Edmundsbury Press, 1993.


INDIAN

Buitenen, J. A. B. van. *Mahabharata,* vols. 1 and 2. Chicago: University of Chicago Press, 1973.

Cavendish, Richard. *Mythology.* New York: Rizzoli, 1980.

Keith, A. Berriedale. *Indian Mythology,* vol. 6, *Mythology of All Races,* ed. J. C. MacCulloch. New York: Cooper Square Publishers, 1964.

O'Flaherty, W. D. *Hindu Myths.* New York: Penguin, 1975.

Subramaniam, Kamala. *Ramayana.* Bombay: Bharatiya Vidya Bhavan, 1983.


JAPANESE

Anesaki, Masaharu. *Japanese Mythology,* vol. 8, *Mythology of All Races,* ed. J. C. MacCulloch. New York: Cooper Square Publishers, 1964.

Seki, Keigo. *Folktales of Japan.* Chicago: University of Chicago Press, 1963.


NATIVE AMERICAN

Alexander, Hartley B. *North American Mythology,* vol. 10, *Mythology of All Races,* ed. J. C. MacCulloch. New York: Cooper Square Publishers, 1964.

Parsons, E. C. *Pueblo Indian Religion.* Chicago: University of Chicago Press, 1939.

Spence, Lewis. *Myths and Legends of the North American Indian.* London: Harrap, 1914.

# ACKNOWLEDGMENTS

For help and research I am indebted to Judy Levin, Andrew J. D. Bowman, and Brian K. Styles, Mary Fletcher, Barrie Kavasch, and Tanya Pond, who gathered information for this book from the following places: New York Society Library; New York Public Library; Neilson Library, Smith College; Institute of Native American Studies; Marion and Knox County, Ohio, Libraries; Ohio State University; Selover Public Library in Chesterville, Ohio; and the Internet. Special thanks to Paul Pontois for calling my attention to a number of excellent stories involving French female warriors, which may find their way into a subsequent collection. Thanks also to my editor, Andrea Schneeman, for her ongoing support.

# INDEX

from the Celtic deities **Morrigan** and Macha. She first appears in Geoffrey of Monmouth's *Vita Merlini* as an immortal from the Isle of Avalon valued for her powers in healing and the magic arts; later writers made her the half sister of **King Arthur.** Over the centuries Morgan's character was distorted and debased.

Morrigan, 8, 10, 39–41; Celtic goddess of war, sometimes known as Queen of Nightmares. Morrigan often appears with her sisters, Bodb (also a war goddess) and Macha (the horse goddess), depicted as warlike furies or crows who urge warriors to fight. In *The History of Ireland,* by John Keating, all three sisters are goddesses of an ancient Faerie race believed to be some of the earliest settlers in Ireland.

Mu Lan, 11; maiden of Chinese folklore who disguised herself as a warrior so she could save her father from combat

Nero, 51; first-century Roman tyrant infamous for many acts of cruelty during his reign

Ng Nui, 11; nun turned warrior who created a martial art form called Shaolin Temple boxing (lived around 1600)

Nineveh, 23; one of the oldest cities in ancient Assyria; on the Tigris River

Nzinga Mbande, 8, 10; African leader of territories on the frontier of Angola who, with the help of her two sisters, resisted Portuguese colonialism. Thirty-five years of fighting finally won her a peace treaty with the Europeans. She lived 1583–1663.

Olga, 10; after the Barbarians killed her husband, King Igor of Russia, Olga assumed the throne and sought revenge against those responsible. In 955 she introduced Greek Orthodox Christianity to her country. She lived 890–969.

Orithya, 27; the most famous of the Amazon queens, known for her beauty and military skill; daughter and heir to Queen **Marpesia**

Palmyra, 8; during the third century in Arabia, a wealthy city that lay at the center of an important trade route

Penthesilea, 27; queen who led the **Amazons** in the Trojan War against the Athenians. During battle, she was killed by Achilles, and after her death the power and prestige of the Amazons declined.

*Puranas,* 13; a group of eighteen Hindu epics

Rangada (Malha), 10, 16–19; Hindu warrior who led her people through successful hunts and battles

Raziya, 10; sultana of Delhi, once the most powerful state in India (died 1240)

Sanskrit, 13; ancient classical language of India and of Hinduism

Sarka, 10; ancient warrior who led a company of Teutonic knights. A district in Czechoslovakia is named for her.

Scathach, 7, 10, 30–36, 41; Celtic warrior

goddess, inspiration for the **Lady Lochlyn**

Schwarze Hofmannin, 10; also known as Black Farm Woman, she successfully defended her village from attack (lived around 1525)

Scotland, 10, 31–36, 43; the northern peninsula of the isle of Britain

Semiramis, 8, 10, 20–24; semilegendary queen of Assyria, founder of the Golden City of Babylon

Septimia Zenobia, 8, 10; third-century queen of Palmyra. She marched on Egypt, conquering it and half of Asia Minor. When she declared Palmyra independent from the ruling Romans, Emperor Aurelian challenged and conquered the ambitious queen; but instead of taking her life, he provided Zenobia with a palace in which to live out her life in luxury.

Severn, 48–49; illegitimate daughter of **Locrin** by **Estrildis.** The river that divides Wales from England is named for her.

Shiva, 13; foremost Hindu god

Sinjang Halmoni, 11; Korean war goddess

Skye, isle of, 31; island off northwest Scotland

Stonehenge, 53; an arrangement of massive standing stones, originally erected in England about 3000 B.C. for an uncertain purpose

Stour, 47; river in southeastern England

Syria, 21; country located at the eastern end of the Mediterranean Sea, south of Turkey

Tamara, 10; ruler of Georgia (country south of Russia) for thirty-four years, she established a dynasty that prevailed for two and a half centuries (lived 1156–1212)

Tasca, 51, 53; warrior daughter of **Boadicea**

Teoyamiqui, 11; Aztec war goddess

Troy, 51; ancient city in northwestern Asia Minor, besieged by Greeks during the legendary Trojan War

Turkey, 10, 25; country that bridges southwest Asia and southeast Europe

Victory, 52; Greek and Roman winged goddess of victory in war, as well as the victory over one's own ego that leads to wisdom (Nike in Greek myth, Victoria in Roman myth)

Virgil's *Aeneid,* 8; great epic written by a first-century Roman poet about the Trojan War

Winyan Ohitika (Makhta), 11, 66–69; legendary daughter of a Sioux chief who avenged her brothers' deaths

Wounded Knee, battle of, 67; battle between United States troops and the Sioux during which a devastating number of the Native Americans were massacred (1890)

Yakami, 8, 11, 60–64; legendary Japanese girl who slew a sea monster

Yim Wing Chun, 11; Chinese nun who developed her own system of martial arts; pupil of **Ng Nui**

Zimbabwe, 8, 10, 55–59; southeastern African country